何 不 浅 尝 辄 止
joy of first glimpse

浅尝诗丛

蝴蝶的笑声
时光中的女性诗歌
·中英双语·

［英］艾米莉·勃朗特 等 著
凤凰诗歌出版中心 编　程旗 译
江苏凤凰文艺出版社

图书在版编目（CIP）数据

蝴蝶的笑声：时光中的女性诗歌/（英）艾米莉·勃朗特等著；程旗译.——南京：江苏凤凰文艺出版社，2023.7

（浅尝诗丛）

ISBN 978-7-5594-7652-4

Ⅰ.①蝴… Ⅱ.①艾… ②程… Ⅲ.①诗集–世界 Ⅳ.①I12

中国国家版本馆CIP数据核字(2023)第051542号

蝴蝶的笑声：时光中的女性诗歌

（英）艾米莉·勃朗特等 著；程旗 译

出 版 人	张在健
责任编辑	王娱瑶 徐 辰
特约编辑	韩馨雨
装帧设计	徐芳芳
责任印制	刘 巍
出版发行	江苏凤凰文艺出版社
	南京市中央路165号，邮编：210009
出版社网址	http://www.jswenyi.com
印 刷	江苏凤凰新华印务集团有限公司
开 本	880毫米×1230毫米 1/32
印 张	6.75
字 数	110千字
版 次	2023年7月第1版 2023年7月第1次印刷
标准书号	ISBN 978-7-5594-7652-4
定 价	42.00元

江苏凤凰文艺版图书凡印刷、装订错误，可向出版社调换，联系电话025-83280257

CONTENT 目录

Emily Brontë

[英国]艾米莉·勃朗特

002　Love and Friendship
003　爱情与友谊

004　Fall, Leaves, Fall
005　秋天，树叶，飘落

006　Stanzas
007　诗节

008　The Night Is Darkening Round Me
009　我周围夜色渐浓

010　Often Rebuked, yet always Back Returning
012　常被责备，却一再回归

Elizabeth Barrett Browning

[英国] 伊丽莎白·巴雷特·勃朗宁

016　Love
017　爱

018　Sonnets from the Portuguese 35:
　　　If I Leave All for Thee, Wilt Thou Exchange
019　《葡萄牙人的十四行诗》第 35 首：
　　　如果我把一切交给你，你可愿交换

020　Sonnets from the Portuguese 38:
　　　First Time He Kissed Me, He but Only Kissed
021　《葡萄牙人的十四行诗》第 38 首：
　　　第一次吻我，他只吻了……

022　Sonnets from the Portuguese 44:
　　　Beloved, Thou Has Brought Me Many Flowers
023　《葡萄牙人的十四行诗》第 44 首：
　　　亲爱的，你已送我那么多花

024　A Musical Instrument
027　一只乐器

Emily Dickinson

［美国］艾米莉·狄金森

032　I Would Not Paint — a Picture —
034　我不想绘——一幅画——

036　A Bird, Came Down the Walk—
038　一只小鸟，沿小径走来

040　If You Were Coming in the Fall
042　如果你在秋天到来

044　Summer Shower
045　夏日阵雨

046　Called Back
048　召回

050　The Lovers
051　爱人

Hilda Doolittle
[美国] 希尔达·杜利特尔

054　Oread
055　山林仙女

056　The Garden
058　花园

060　Evening
061　黄昏

062　Moonrise
063　月升

064　Nails for Petals
066　钉子花瓣

068　Flute Song
069　笛之歌

Amy Lowell
[美国] 艾米·洛威尔

072　Song
074　歌

076　Petals
077　花瓣

078　Behind a Wall
080　围墙之后

082　Listening
083　听

084　Granadilla
085　西番莲

Katherine Mansfield

[新西兰] 凯瑟琳·曼斯菲尔德

088　Butterfly Laughter
089　蝴蝶的笑声

090　The Awakening River
092　苏醒的河流

093　Voices of the Air
094　空中的叫声

095　Fairy Tale
096　神话故事

097　The Quarrel
098　争吵

Edna St. Vincent Millay

[美国] 埃德娜·圣·文森特·米莱

100　Figs from Thistles
101　蒺藜中长出的无花果

102　I Think I Should Have Loved You Presently
103　我想我应该马上就算爱过你了

104　Witch-Wife
105　巫妻

106　Spring
107　春

108　City Trees
109　城市的树

Marianne Moore

[美国] 玛丽安娜·穆尔

112 He Made This Screen
113 他制作了这座屏风

114 Roses Only
116 只有玫瑰

118 That Harp You Play so Well
119 那竖琴你弹得真好

120 Those Various Scalpels
123 那些各式各样的手术刀

125 To an Intra-mural Rat
126 致一只墙内的老鼠

127 An Egyptian Pulled Glass Bottle in the Shape of a Fish
128 一个鱼形的埃及拉制玻璃瓶

Christina Rossetti

[英国]克丽丝蒂娜·罗塞蒂

130 From Sunset to Star Rise
131 从日落到星起

132 A Birthday
133 生日

134 A Summer Wish
136 夏日心愿

138 Echo
139 回声

140 Another Spring
142 又一个春天

144 "One Foot on Sea, and One on Shore"
146 "一脚踩在海上,一脚踏在岸边"

Sappho

[古希腊] 萨福

150　It's no Use / Mother Dear...
151　没用啊 / 亲爱的妈妈……

152　As Wind Upon the Mountain Oaks
153　像狂风撼动橡树

154　One Girl
155　一位少女

156　Aphrodite's Doves
158　阿芙洛狄忒的鸽子

160　Leda
161　丽达

Sara Teasdale

[美国] 萨拉·提斯黛尔

164 Let It Be Forgotten
165 忘记它

166 What Do I Care
167 我有何在意

168 Only in Sleep
169 只在睡梦中

170 The Mystery
171 秘密

172 May Day
173 五朔节

174 Thoughts
176 想法

Elinor Wylie

[美国]埃莉诺·怀利

180 The Lion and the Lamb
182 狮子与羔羊

184 Sunset on the Spire
186 尖塔上的日落

188 Escape
189 逃跑

190 Silver Filigree
191 银丝饰品

192 Velvet Shoes
194 天鹅绒鞋

196 The Persian Kitten
198 波斯猫

Emily Brontë
[英国]艾米莉·勃朗特

1818—1848

她是《呼啸山庄》的作者艾米莉·勃朗特。她的姐姐夏洛特以《简·爱》而闻名,妹妹安妮写下《艾格尼丝·格雷》。三姐妹都英年早逝,在英国文学史上留下了传奇。艾米莉的诗歌热情奔放、真挚动人。

Love and Friendship

Love is like the wild rose-briar,

Friendship like the holly-tree—

The holly is dark when the rose-briar blooms

But which will bloom most constantly?

The wild rose-briar is sweet in spring,

Its summer blossoms scent the air;

Yet wait till winter comes again

And who will call the wild-briar fair?

Then scorn the silly rose-wreath now

And deck thee with the holly's sheen,

That when December blights thy brow

He still may leave thy garland green.

爱情与友谊

爱情像丛野蔷薇,
友谊像棵冬青树——
当蔷薇绽放明艳,冬青阴沉晦暗
哪个才能长久繁茂、四季葱郁?

春天　蔷薇楚楚惹人怜爱,
夏天　花朵盛放传送芬芳;
然而　待冬季再次来临
谁还会称颂它的美丽模样?

因此现在就舍弃可笑的蔷薇花环
用冬青的光泽把自己装扮,
当严冬的苦寒让你愁眉不展
冬青花冠依旧绿意盎然。

Fall, Leaves, Fall

Fall, leaves, fall; die, flowers, away;

Lengthen night and shorten day;

Every leaf speaks bliss to me

Fluttering from the autumn tree.

I shall smile when wreaths of snow

Blossom where the rose should grow;

I shall sing when night's decay

Ushers in a drearier day.

秋天,树叶,飘落

秋叶飘落,花朵凋谢;

黑夜渐长　白昼缩短;

每片叶子都向我吐露祝福

翩翩飘落秋树。

当白雪桂冠绽放在玫瑰生长之处

我应该微笑;

当黑夜衰减开启越发阴沉的一天

我应该歌唱。

Stanzas

I'll not weep that thou art going to leave me,
There's nothing lovely here;
And doubly will the dark world grieve me,
While thy heart suffers there.

I'll not weep, because the summer's glory
Must always end in gloom;
And, follow out the happiest story—
It closes with a tomb!

And I am weary of the anguish
Increasing winters bear;
Weary to watch the spirit languish
Through years of dead despair.

So, if a tear, when thou art dying,
Should haply fall from me,
It is but that my soul is sighing,
To go and rest with thee.

诗 节

我不会因你将离去而哭泣,
这里已没什么值得眷恋;
黑暗的世界将予我双倍的哀伤,
若你的心在那忍受苦楚。

我不会哭泣,因为夏季的光辉
必将以昏暗结束;
跟随最幸福的故事走向——
结局却是一座坟墓!

漫长的冬季滋生创痛,
这创痛已让我生厌;
厌倦再看到心灵熬煎
在彻骨绝望里终年。

因此,当你命已垂危,
也许我会流下一滴眼泪,
这只是我的灵魂在叹息,
想与你同归长眠之地。

The Night Is Darkening Round Me

The night is darkening round me,

The wild winds coldly blow;

But a tyrant spell has bound me,

And I cannot, cannot go.

The giant trees are bending,

Their bare boughs weighed with snow;

The storm is fast descending,

And yet I cannot go.

Clouds beyond clouds above me,

Wastes beyond wastes below;

But nothing drear can move me;

I will not, cannot go.

我周围夜色渐浓

我周围夜色渐浓,

狂风在凄厉怒吼;

但我被暴虐的符咒束缚,

使我不能,不能离开。

巨大的树木身姿佝偻,

干枯的粗枝将积雪承受;

暴风雪将迅速降临,

但我仍旧不能离开。

头顶是一层层阴云,

脚下是一重重荒原;

可任何忧郁都不能挪动我,

我既不会,也不能离开。

Often Rebuked, yet always Back Returning

Often rebuked, yet always back returning
    To those first feelings that were born with me,
And leaving busy chase of wealth and learning
    For idle dreams of things which cannot be:

To-day, I will seek not the shadowy region;
    Its unsustaining vastness waxes drear;
And visions rising, legion after legion,
    Bring the unreal world too strangely near.

I'll walk, but not in old heroic traces,
    And not in paths of high morality,
And not among the half-distinguished faces,
    The clouded forms of long-past history.

I'll walk where my own nature would be leading:
    It vexes me to choose another guide:
Where the gray flocks in ferny glens are feeding;

Where the wild wind blows on the mountain side.

What have those lonely mountains worth revealing?
　More glory and more grief than I can tell:
The earth that wakes one human heart to feeling
　Can centre both the worlds of Heaven and Hell.

常被责备,却一再回归

常被责备,但却一再回归
我与生俱来的初心本愿,
远离对财富学识的迫切追寻
沉浸在空中楼阁的渺茫梦境。

如今我不再找寻阴影之域;
那无垠的广袤　愈增沉闷忧郁;
幻像数不胜数,重重浮现,
将虚幻世界拉近　仿若眼前。

我将前行,但不追随过去英雄的踪迹,
也不遵循为人称颂的崇高德行,
不希求跻身那些依稀可辨的显赫面孔,
那些久远历史中的模糊身影。

我将前行,顺遂自己天性的引领:
另选其他向导将为我徒增烦扰:
那里 灰白牧群在多蕨的幽谷觅食;
那里 狂野的风在山边啸叫。

这群山孤寂冷清　怎会值得深省?
其荣耀和哀苦　让我难以尽数:
那唤醒人心感悟的大地
让天堂和地狱在此中心会集。

Elizabeth Barrett Browning
［英国］伊丽莎白·巴雷特·勃朗宁
1806—1861

在 19 世纪的英语世界，伊丽莎白·巴雷特·勃朗宁是一位拥有至高地位的女性诗人，她被称为"勃朗宁夫人"。体弱多病的她在 39 岁那年结识了小她 6 岁的诗人罗伯特·勃朗宁，由此写下许多动人的情诗。她对诗歌界影响深远，她的画像就挂在艾米莉·狄金森的卧室。

Love

We cannot live, except thus mutually

We alternate, aware or unaware,

The reflex act of life: and when we bear

Our virtue onward most impulsively,

Most full of invocation, and to be

Most instantly compellant, certes, there

We live most life, whoever breathes most air

And counts his dying years by sun and sea.

But when a soul, by choice and conscience, doth

Throw out her full force on another soul,

The conscience and the concentration both

Make mere life, Love. For Life in perfect whole

And aim consummated, is Love in sooth,

As nature's magnet-heat rounds pole with pole.

爱

我们无法生存,除非像这样互换
我们交换生命的本能反应,
有意或无意:我们怀抱美德前行
在最冲动、最满心祈求、
最紧急迫切之时,依然如此
谁呼吸最多空气,谁的人生就最久长
在太阳下大海边数点剩余的时光。
但当一个灵魂,出于自愿或良知,
将全部心力倾注于另一个灵魂,
这种良知和专注都将空乏的人生,
转化为爱。因为让人生圆满
让目标实现,才是真正的爱,
像自然界的磁热　一极绕向另一极。

Sonnets from the Portuguese 35: If I Leave All for Thee, Wilt Thou Exchange

If I leave all for thee, wilt thou exchange
And be all to me? Shall I never miss
Home-talk and blessing and the common kiss
That comes to each in turn, nor count it strange,
When I look up, to drop on a new range
Of walls and floors ... another home than this?
Nay, wilt thou fill that place by me which is
Filled by dead eyes too tender to know change?
That's hardest. If to conquer love, has tried,
To conquer grief, tries more ... as all things prove;
For grief indeed is love and grief beside.
Alas, I have grieved so I am hard to love.
Yet love me—wilt thou? Open thine heart wide,
And fold within, the wet wings of thy dove.

《葡萄牙人的十四行诗》第35首：
如果我把一切交给你，你可愿交换

如果我把一切交给你，你可愿交换，

成为我的一切？我是否就再不会怀念

家常聊天、祝福和日常亲吻，

那些彼此轮流给予的东西？也不会觉得陌生，

当我抬头，目光落处是一片新的

墙壁和地板……与此间不同的另一个家？

不，你可愿填补我身旁的位置？

那曾柔情深种、心意不变的双眼

此刻已然长眠。

这可千难万难。如果说征服爱情尚可尝试，

征服悲伤要试更多次……世事早已证实；

因为悲伤其实就是爱但又增添了悲伤。

哎，我已历经悲伤所以爱我很难。

但爱我吧——你可愿意？把你的心敞开些，

让你那打湿了双翅的鸽子，进来收翼安憩。

Sonnets from the Portuguese 38: First Time He Kissed Me, He but Only Kissed

First time he kissed me, he but only kissed
The fingers of this hand wherewith I write,
And ever since it grew more clean and white.
Slow to world-greetings, quick with its "O, list,"
When the angels speak. A ring of amethyst
I could not wear here, plainer to my sight,
Than that first kiss. The second passed in height
The first, and sought the forehead, and half missed,
Half falling on the hair. O beyond meed!
That was the chrism of love, which love's own crown,
With sanctifying sweetness, did precede.
The third, upon my lips, was folded down
In perfect, purple state; since when, indeed,
I have been proud and said, "My Love, my own."

《葡萄牙人的十四行诗》第 38 首：
第一次吻我,他只吻了……

第一次吻我,他只吻了

我提笔书写的手指,

从此它变得愈发洁净白皙……

轻慢俗世的召唤……而敏于记叙

天使述说的吉光片羽。紫水晶戒指,

我无法佩戴在这里,跟初吻相比,

它太过朴素无奇。第二次吻,超越了

初次的高度,它找寻前额,但略有偏斜,

一半落上发丝。哦这超额的奖赏!

这是爱的圣油,在这之前,

圣洁芬芳的爱之王冠,已经加冕。

第三次吻,叠印在我唇上,

如此完美、庄重高贵!自此以后,的确,

我开始变得骄傲并宣称:"我的爱人,我自己的。"

Sonnets from the Portuguese 44: Beloved, Thou Has Brought Me Many Flowers

Beloved, thou hast brought me many flowers

Plucked in the garden, all the summer through

And winter, and it seemed as if they grew

In this close room, nor missed the sun and showers,

So, in the like name of that love of ours,

Take back these thoughts which here unfolded too,

And which on warm and cold days I withdrew

From my heart's ground. Indeed, those beds and bowers

Be overgrown with bitter weeds and rue,

And wait thy weeding; yet here's eglantine,

Here's ivy!— take them, as I used to do

Thy flowers, and keep them where they shall not pine.

Instruct thine eyes to keep their colours true,

And tell thy soul, their roots are left in mine.

《葡萄牙人的十四行诗》第 44 首：
亲爱的，你已送我那么多花

亲爱的，你已送我那么多花

从花园里采摘，整个夏季到冬季

都不曾停歇，它们看上去好像

能够在这幽闭的房间生长，

并不缺少阳光照拂和雨露滋养，

那么同样，以我们的爱情之名，

我收回这些将在此剖白的念想，

在温暖或寒冷的日子里，

它们曾在我心田上摇晃。

的确，我那里的花圃和树荫

长满了苦辛的野草和芸香，

等待你来剪除；但这里也有野蔷薇，

也有常春藤！——收下它们，就像我曾

收下你的花，好生保管别让它们凋萎。

精心照看勿令它们失色，

并告诉你的心灵，它们的根茎深埋在我心中。

A Musical Instrument

I.

WHAT was he doing, the great god Pan,

Down in the reeds by the river?

Spreading ruin and scattering ban,

Splashing and paddling with hoofs of a goat,

And breaking the golden lilies afloat

With the dragon-fly on the river.

II.

He tore out a reed, the great god Pan,

From the deep cool bed of the river:

The limpid water turbidly ran,

And the broken lilies a-dying lay,

And the dragon-fly had fled away,

Ere he brought it out of the river.

III.

High on the shore sat the great god Pan,

While turbidly flowed the river;

And hacked and hewed as a great god can,

With his hard bleak steel at the patient reed,

Till there was not a sign of a leaf indeed

To prove it fresh from the river.

IV.

He cut it short, did the great god Pan,

(How tall it stood in the river!)

Then drew the pith, like the heart of a man,

Steadily from the outside ring,

And notched the poor dry empty thing

In holes, as he sat by the river.

V.

"This is the way," laughed the great god Pan,

(Laughed while he sat by the river),

"The only way, since gods began

To make sweet music, they could succeed."

Then, dropping his mouth to a hole in the reed,

He blew in power by the river.

VI.

Sweet, sweet, sweet, O Pan!

Piercing sweet by the river!

Blinding sweet, O great god Pan!

The sun on the hill forgot to die,

And the lilies revived, and the dragon-fly

Came back to dream on the river.

VII.

Yet half a beast is the great god Pan,

To laugh as he sits by the river,

Making a poet out of a man:

The true gods sigh for the cost and pain, —

For the reed which grows nevermore again

As a reed with the reeds in the river.

一只乐器

（一）

他在做什么，伟大的潘神，

在河边的芦苇丛中？

传播毁灭和散布禁令，

用山羊蹄拨水泼溅，

打破河面上漂浮的

栖着蜻蜓的金色睡莲。

（二）

他撕裂一支芦苇，伟大的潘神，

从幽深清凉的河床：

清澈的河水浑浊流淌，

破碎的睡莲垂死躺倒，

那只蜻蜓　在被他从河里捞出前

已经逃跑。

（三）

伟大的潘神坐在高高的岸上，

而浑浊的河水正流淌：

正如一个伟大的神祇,他用坚硬冰冷的钢铁

对忍耐的苇丛又劈又砍,

直到再无一片苇叶看上去

还留有清新出水的姿态。

(四)

他将芦苇割短,伟大的潘神,

(它本在河里高高站立!)

他从外圈稳稳地拔出髓心,

像掏出一个人的心脏,

他坐在河边,把这可怜的空心干枯物

刻出圆孔。

(五)

"就是这么做",伟大的潘神笑了,

(他坐在河边大笑,)

"唯一的做法,只要神想要制造

美妙的音乐,他们就能成功。"

然后,把嘴巴贴近芦苇的圆孔,

他开始在河边吹奏。

（六）

美妙，美妙，美妙啊，潘！

河边的音乐，美妙得铭心入骨！

美妙得令人炫目，哦　伟大的潘神！

山边的太阳忘记西沉，

睡莲起死回生，蜻蜓飞回

落在河面上做梦。

（七）

但坐在河边大笑的　伟大的潘神，

不过是一个半兽，

别把凡夫俗子错认作诗人：

真正的神灵会叹息代价沉痛——

为那支永不再生长的芦苇

它曾生长在河中的苇丛。

Emily Dickinson
[美国]艾米莉·狄金森
1830—1886

艾米莉·狄金森出生于19世纪的美国,她被誉为公元前7世纪萨福以来西方最杰出的女诗人。她过着神秘的、隐居般的安静日子,生前发表过的诗歌不足10首,大部分动人的诗篇都被锁在盒子里,直到她去世数年之后才被发现。她与惠特曼一起,被并称为美国现代派诗歌的先驱。她在迷人的孤独感里,倾听着世界的脉搏,描画着女性的灵魂。

I Would Not Paint — a Picture —

I would not paint — a picture —

I'd rather be the One

It's bright impossibility

To dwell — delicious — on —

And wonder how the fingers feel

Whose rare — celestial — stir —

Evokes so sweet a torment —

Such sumptuous — Despair —

I would not talk, like Cornets —

I'd rather be the One

Raised softly to the Ceilings —

And out, and easy on —

Through Villages of Ether —

Myself endued Balloon

By but a lip of Metal —

The pier to my Pontoon —

Nor would I be a Poet —

It's finer — Own the Ear —

Enamored — impotent — content —

The License to revere,

A privilege so awful

What would the Dower be,

Had I the Art to stun myself

With Bolts — of Melody!

我不想绘——一幅画——

我不想绘——一幅画——

我更想成为那人

去明亮的超凡出世之地

——美妙地——栖居

并好奇指尖有何感受

其珍奇罕见——飘逸若仙的——搅动

唤起如此甜蜜的折磨——

如此奢侈的——绝望——

我不想,像短号那样讲话——

我更想成为它

被轻柔送上屋顶——

飘出,再徐徐上升——

穿越云霄的村落——

我化身一颗气球

只需经由一枚金属嘴——

那通向我浮船的码头

我也不想做什么诗人——

洗耳恭听——更好——

沉迷——无力——满足——

表达敬畏的资格,

多么傲人的特权。

若我能凭借旋律的——闪电

震撼自己,

这该是怎样的天分啊!

A Bird, Came Down the Walk—

A Bird, came down the Walk—

He did not know I saw—

He bit an Angle Worm in halves

And ate the fellow, raw,

And then, he drank a Dew

From a convenient Grass—

And then hopped sidewise to the Wall

To let a Beetle pass—

He glanced with rapid eyes,

That hurried all abroad—

They looked like frightened Beads, I thought,

He stirred his Velvet Head.—

Like one in danger, Cautious,

I offered him a Crumb,

And he unrolled his feathers,

And rowed him softer Home—

Than Oars divide the Ocean,

Too silver for a seam,

Or Butterflies, off Banks of Noon,

Leap, plashless as they swim.

一只小鸟,沿小径走来

一只小鸟,沿小径走来——
不知道已被我看见——
他把一条蚯蚓撕咬成两段,
然后将它生吞活咽,

随后,他从近旁草叶上
啄饮了一滴露珠——
便蹦跳向一旁的墙边,
给一只甲虫让出通路——

他的双眼滴溜乱转,
快速扫视四面八方——
看起来像受惊的珠子,
毛绒绒的脑袋晃了又晃——

像身处危险、小心翼翼,
我投给他面包渣一粒,
他便张开了翅膀,
划向家的方向——

比桨分开海水更轻柔,

银色的波纹无痕合拢,

或蝴蝶,从正午的岸边飞跃而下,

振翅悠游,击水无声。

If You Were Coming in the Fall

If you were coming in the fall,
I'd brush the summer by
With half a smile and half a spurn,
As housewives do a fly.

If I could see you in a year,
I'd wind the months in balls—
And put them each in separate drawers,
For fear the numbers fuse—

If only centuries delayed,
I'd count them on my hand,
Subtracting till my fingers dropped
Into Van Diemen's land.

If certain, when this life was out—
That yours and mine should be,
I'd toss it yonder like a rind,
And take eternity—

But now, uncertain of the length

Of this, that is between,

It goads me, like the goblin bee—

That will not state — its sting.

如果你在秋天到来

如果你在秋天到来,
我会把夏天轻轻拂去
半带微笑、半带弃绝,
像主妇将苍蝇驱逐。

如果一年内能见到你,
我会把月份缠绕成团,
然后放进分隔的抽屉,
以防它们纠结混乱。

如果只推迟了几个世纪,
我会用手将它们数计,
删删减减直至我的指尖
坠入世界尽头的荒原。

如果确定,待此生将尽,
你我的生命才能相亲,
我会把生命像果皮远丢,
去体味永恒不朽。

但现在,全然无法估量

要等待的时间有多长,

这令我烦恼心煎,像妖蜂,

将它的毒刺隐而不宣。

注:

  Van Diemen's land,现在的塔斯马尼亚岛。16世纪,荷兰航海家 Abel Tasman 发现该岛并将之命名为 Van Diemen's land。后英国人在这里修建阴森的监狱,并作为流放之地。有人间地狱、死亡之地、世界尽头的喻意。

Summer Shower

A drop fell on the apple tree,
Another on the roof;
A half a dozen kissed the eaves,
And made the gables laugh.

A few went out to help the brook,
That went to help the sea.
Myself conjectured, Were they pearls,
What necklaces could be!

The dust replaced in hoisted roads,
The birds jocoser sung;
The sunshine threw his hat away,
The orchards spangles hung.

The breezes brought dejected lutes,
And bathed them in the glee;
The East put out a single flag,
And signed the fete away.

夏日阵雨

一滴落在苹果树，

一滴落到屋顶；

五六点亲吻屋檐，

让山墙绽放笑颜。

一些出走去助力溪流，

又一路前行汇入大海。

设想它们若是珍珠，

这该是怎样一条项链！

飞扬路面的尘土被涤荡，

鸟儿们滑稽可笑地鸣唱；

阳光甩掉了遮头的云帽，

果园里悬挂着无数晶莹光片。

微风吹来低落的琴音，

让它们在欢欣中沐浴；

东方升起一面旗帜，

宣布这场游乐终止。

Called Back

Just lost when I was saved!

Just felt the world go by!

Just girt me for the onset with eternity,

When breath blew back,

And on the other side

I heard recede the disappointed tide!

Therefore, as one returned, I feel,

Odd secrets of the line to tell!

Some sailor, skirting foreign shores,

Some pale reporter from the awful doors

Before the seal!

Next time, to stay!

Next time, the things to see

By ear unheard,

Unscrutinized by eye.

Next time, to tarry,

While the ages steal, —

Slow tramp the centuries,

And the cycles wheel.

召 回

当我获救时,只觉怅然若失!

只觉世界从我身边流逝!

永恒刚要开始　就把我束缚,

当呼吸开始回复,

而另一边

失望的潮水在声声消退!

因此,作为回归者,我想披露,

有关边界线的奇诡秘闻!

作为绕过了陌生海岸的水手,

于封印之前

走出可畏之门的　面色惨白的报告人!

下一次,要留下!

下一次,要对所见之事

充耳不闻、

闭目不察。

下一次,要等候,

待岁月悄悄流走——

漫漫跋涉　直至世纪更替，

循环轮转。

The Lovers

The rose did caper on her cheek,
Her bodice rose and fell,
Her pretty speech, like drunken men,
Did stagger pitiful.

Her fingers fumbled at her work, —
Her needle would not go;
What ailed so smart a little maid
It puzzled me to know,

Till opposite I spied a cheek
That bore another rose;
Just opposite, another speech
That like the drunkard goes;

A vest that, like the bodice, danced
To the immortal tune, —
Till those two troubled little clocks
Ticked softly into one.

爱 人

玫瑰在她脸颊上欢跃,
她的胸衣起伏不断,
可爱的言语,像是醉汉,
结结巴巴、惹人爱怜。

她的手指在胡乱摸索——
她的针脚也不再游走;
这机灵的姑娘为何如此窘迫,
让我满心好奇疑惑。

直到我发现对面的脸颊
绽放着另一朵玫瑰花;
就在对面,这另一人的言语
也同样像是个醉汉;

这副马甲,也像那胸衣,
随不朽的曲调起伏舞蹈——
直到这两只困扰的小小钟表
嘀嗒声轻柔地融为一体。

Hilda Doolittle
[美国]希尔达·杜利特尔
1886—1961

希尔达·杜利特尔是美国第一代现代派诗人，通常被称为 H.D.。她钟情希腊诗歌，擅长浓缩语言和捕捉意象，笔下的文字富有音乐性。她多情、大胆、前卫，是同辈作家的宠儿，更是后辈诗人的偶像。H.D. 曾经的情人庞德为她发明了"意象派"这个专有名词，也使她被公认为典型的意象派诗人。

Oread

Whirl up, sea—

whirl your pointed pines,

splash your great pines

on our rocks,

hurl your green over us,

cover us with your pools of fir.

山林仙女

翻腾吧,大海——
翻卷起你那尖顶的松树,
把你巨大的松涛
飞溅在我们的岩石上,
把你的绿意投掷于我们身上,
用你的一池冷杉覆盖我们。

The Garden

I

You are clear

O rose, cut in rock,

hard as the descent of hail.

I could scrape the colour

from the petals

like spilt dye from a rock.

If I could break you

I could break a tree.

If I could stir

I could break a tree—

I could break you.

II

O wind, rend open the heat,

cut apart the heat,
rend it to tatters.

Fruit cannot drop
through this thick air—
fruit cannot fall into heat
that presses up and blunts
the points of pears
and rounds the grapes.

Cut the heat—
plough through it,
turning it on either side
of your path.

花园

(一)

你很清晰

哦玫瑰,刻在石上,

像降落的冰雹一样坚硬。

我能从花瓣上

刮下颜色

就像从石头上分离颜料。

若我能折断你

我就能折断一棵树。

若我能激昂而起

我就能折断一棵树——

我就能折断你。

(二)

哦风,撕裂这炎热,

切开这炎热,
把它撕成碎片。

果实无法掉落,
穿透这厚重的空气——
果实无法落入炎热,
这炎热鼓胀并磨钝了
梨子的尖头,
又挫圆了葡萄。

切割炎热——
犁过炎热,
把它翻开在
你道路的两侧。

Evening

The light passes
from ridge to ridge,
from flower to flower—
the hepaticas, wide-spread
under the light
grow faint—
the petals reach inward,
the blue tips bend
toward the bluer heart
and the flowers are lost.

The cornel-buds are still white,
but shadows dart
from the cornel-roots—
black creeps from root to root,
each leaf
cuts another leaf on the grass,
shadow seeks shadow,
then both leaf
and leaf-shadow are lost.

黄 昏

光
从山脊传向山脊,
从花朵传向花朵——
遍生山野的蝴蝶花,
在光下
逐渐黯淡模糊——
花瓣向里收拢,
蓝色的蕊尖弯曲
朝向更蓝的花心,
然后花消失不见。

山茱萸的蓓蕾依然莹白,
但是阴影
从它根部猛冲出来——
黑暗从根须蔓延到根须,
每片叶子
切割着草地上的另一片叶,
阴影追寻着阴影,
随后叶子
与叶影　都消失不见。

Moonrise

Will you glimmer on the sea?
Will you fling your spear-head
on the shore?
What note shall we pitch?

We have a song,
on the bank we share our arrows;
the loosed string tells our note:

O flight,
bring her swiftly to our song.
she is great,
we measure her by the pine-trees.

月 升

你是否会在海上闪耀微光?
你是否会把你的银枪头
投掷到海岸?
我们该选定哪个音符的音高?

我们有一首歌,
在岸边我们把箭共享;
让松弛的弦帮我们定调。

哦 飞逝的光阴,
带她快速融入我们的歌,
她那么巨大,
我们用松树来测量她。

Nails for Petals

O, we were penitent enough, God knows,
you wore the Nessus' tunic,[①]
I, the rose with nails for petals,

underneath my robe; I pressed
the seven swords of Mary to my heart,[②]
within the hollow of my wounded breasts;

I walked, numb with the incense,
never passed a friar or priest or brother,
but my glance fell to the pavement,

but the very stones of the cathedral floor
bore imprint of your sandals;
I must close my eyes and stare

at the rose-window, but the rose betrayed,
the glow of green and azure set aflame
the row of kings and saints along the wall.

the stone-story of Creation and the Fall;[3]

O, we were penitent enough, God knows,

but how revoke decrees made long ago?

钉子花瓣

哦,我们已充分忏悔,上帝知道,
你穿着涅索斯的短袍,
我,戴着钉子花瓣的玫瑰,

在我的袍服下面;我将
圣母玛丽亚的七把剑紧贴心脏,
在我受伤胸膛的空腔;

我走着路,被香火熏到麻木,
从未路过一位托钵僧、牧师或教徒,
但我的目光落在那石板路,

就在这教堂地板的石面,
承载着你丑闻的印痕;
我必须闭上眼睛　紧盯住

玫瑰花窗,但玫瑰背叛了信仰,
碧绿和蔚蓝的光芒　辉映出
墙边的那排国王和圣徒。

创世纪和人类堕落的石刻故事；

哦，我们已充分忏悔，上帝知道，

但很久前制定的法令　又要如何撤销？

注：

① Nessus，涅索斯，希腊神话中的半人马，是载人渡冥河的艄公。

② the seven swords of Mary，基督教里，指圣母玛利亚七苦，因耶稣受难而圣心受苦之事。

③ Creation and the Fall，基督教里的上帝创世记和亚当夏娃偷吃禁果堕落人间的故事。

Flute Song

Little scavenger away,

touch not the door,

beat not the portal down,

cross not the sill,

silent until

my song, bright and shrill,

breathes out its lay.

Little scavenger avaunt,

tempt me with jeer and taunt,

yet you will wait to-day;

for it were surely ill

to mock and shout and revel;

it were more fit to tell

with flutes and calathes,

your mother's praise.

笛之歌

小食腐兽走开,
别碰到通道,
别砸开正门,
别越过门槛,
保持安静,直到
我嘹亮尖锐的歌声,
呼出它的吟唱诗篇。

小食腐兽滚开,
用揶揄和奚落怂恿我,
但今天你需要等待;
因为这肯定是病态,
嘲笑、叫喊、狂欢作乐;
更健康的方式
是用笛子和果篮述说,
对母亲的赞歌。

Amy Lowell

[美国]艾米·洛威尔

1874—1925

艾米·洛威尔是一位个性十足的美国女诗人、演员、编辑、译者。她喜欢穿男装,抽雪茄。她热爱中国古典诗歌,是意象派运动的领袖人物之一。她曾说:"上帝把我造就成一个商人,可我让自己成为了诗人。"

Song

Oh! To be a flower
Nodding in the sun,
Bending, then upspringing
As the breezes run;
Holding up
A scent-brimmed cup,
Full of summer's fragrance to the summer sun.

Oh! To be a butterfly
Still, upon a flower,
Winking with its painted wings,
Happy in the hour.
Blossoms hold
Mines of gold
Deep within the farthest heart of each chaliced flower.

Oh! To be a cloud
Blowing through the blue,
Shadowing the mountains,

Rushing loudly through

Valleys deep

Where torrents keep

Always their plunging thunder and their misty arch

of blue.

Oh! To be a wave

Splintering on the sand,

Drawing back, but leaving

Lingeringly the land.

Rainbow light

Flashes bright

Telling tales of coral caves half hid in yellow sand.

Soon they die, the flowers;

Insects live a day;

Clouds dissolve in showers;

Only waves at play

Last forever.

Shall endeavor

Make a sea of purpose mightier than we dream to-

day?

歌

哦！做一朵花

在阳光下微微颔首。

随着微风的吹拂，

弯下腰去、复又弹起；

迎着夏日的艳阳，

擎托着香气四溢的花盏，

充满夏日的芬芳。

哦！做一只蝴蝶

静静地，停歇花上，

鲜艳的翅膀翩然扑闪，

乐享这时辰的怡然。

每只盛开的杯状花朵，

花心最深处　都承满了

黄金的矿藏。

哦！做一片云

被风吹送　浮游蓝天，

遮蔽了群山，

喧闹地冲过　峡谷深处，

那里急流湍鸣

跌宕奔涌声震如雷，

湛蓝的脊背水雾氤氲。

哦！做一点浪花

碎裂在沙滩，

收回脚步，但水印留痕，

在地面留恋地慢慢消散。

虹彩的光线明亮闪烁，

讲述着黄沙半掩下

珊瑚洞穴的传说。

不久它们就死去，那些花朵；

虫儿们朝生暮死；

云彩消散于阵雨；

只有海浪的嬉戏

日以继夜　永不停歇。

不歇的努力，能否造就

比今日之梦想更强大的海洋？

Petals

Life is a stream

On which we strew

Petal by petal the flower of our heart;

The end lost in dream,

They float past our view,

We only watch their glad, early start.

Freighted with hope,

Crimsoned with joy,

We scatter the leaves of our opening rose;

Their widening scope,

Their distant employ,

We never shall know. And the stream as it flows

Sweeps them away,

Each one is gone

Ever beyond into infinite ways.

We alone stay

While years hurry on,

The flower fared forth, though its fragrance still stays.

花　瓣

生命是一条溪流，
我们将心灵花朵的花瓣
片片洒落其上；
结局迷失在梦中，
它们漂出了我们的视线，
我们只看到它们雀跃的初始。

满怀着希望，
因喜悦而绯红，
我们散播玫瑰绽放的花瓣；
它们会传送多广，
它们能漂流多远，
我们永无法知晓。溪水潺潺流淌
将它们卷向远方，
每片都消失不见，
逐水流散、远赴天边。
只剩我们独自留下，
光阴似箭、花朵愈远，
但它的余香，仍留心间。

Behind a Wall

I own a solace shut within my heart,

A garden full of many a quaint delight

And warm with drowsy, poppied sunshine; bright,

Flaming with lilies out of whose cups dart

Shining things

With powdered wings.

Here terrace sinks to terrace, arbors close

The ends of dreaming paths; a wanton wind

Jostles the half-ripe pears, and then, unkind,

Tumbles a-slumber in a pillar rose,

With content

Grown indolent.

By night my garden is o'erhung with gems

Fixed in an onyx setting. Fireflies

Flicker their lanterns in my dazzled eyes.

In serried rows I guess the straight, stiff stems

Of hollyhocks

Against the rocks.

So far and still it is that, listening,

I hear the flowers talking in the dawn;

And where a sunken basin cuts the lawn,

Cinctured with iris, pale and glistening,

The sudden swish

Of a waking fish.

围墙之后

我的心里深锁着一方慰藉,
一座花园　充满着乐事奇趣,
阳光和暖迷醉、催人欲眠;
百合明亮耀眼、娇艳欲燃,
花朵杯盏里飞跃出
翅膀敷粉的闪亮生灵。

这里,梯地层层沉接,凉亭临近
梦中小径的尽头;恣意嬉闹的风
推挤着半熟的青梨,又恶劣地
绊翻了一棵攀柱玫瑰的睡梦,
才带着惯有的懒散
心满意足离去。

入夜,我的花园悬垂着宝石
镶嵌在玛瑙板。萤火虫
摇曳着提灯,光彩炫目。
笔直而坚韧的蜀葵,我猜,
正密集成排地抵住岩块。

它如此偏远幽寂,侧耳伫立,
我听到花儿在曙光中笑谈;
还有草地中沉陷的一汪池塘,
环生着鸢尾花,浅淡素雅、水润莹亮,
一尾苏醒的鱼
从中倏然游过。

Listening

'T is you that are the music, not your song.

The song is but a door which, opening wide,

Lets forth the pent-up melody inside,

Your spirit's harmony, which clear and strong

Sings but of you. Throughout your whole life long

Your songs, your thoughts, your doings, each divide

This perfect beauty; waves within a tide,

Or single notes amid a glorious throng.

The song of earth has many different chords;

Ocean has many moods and many tones

Yet always ocean. In the damp Spring woods

The painted trillium smiles, while crisp pine cones

Autumn alone can ripen. So is this

One music with a thousand cadences.

听

你本身就是音乐,不是你的歌唱。
歌声不过是道敞开的门,
释放出内心郁积的旋律,
你心灵的和声,清晰有力
只歌唱你。你整个生命历程中的
每次歌唱、思想、所作所为,都分担了
这完满无瑕的美,如潮汐中的浪花一点点,
如辉煌交响的音符一枚枚。
大地之歌有众多不同的和弦;
海洋也有多种多样的情绪和音调
但它永远是海洋。春季潮湿的林地里
鲜亮的延龄草在微笑,而松脆的松果
只有秋季能把它催熟。同样
你这支音乐,也有千百种韵律。

Granadilla

I cut myself upon the thought of you

And yet I come back to it again and again,

A kind of fury makes me want to draw you out

From the dimness of the present

And set you sharply above me in a wheel of roses.

Then, going obviously to inhale their fragrance,

I touch the blade of you and cling upon it,

And only when the blood runs out across my fingers

Am I at all satisfied.

西番莲

一想起你,我就割伤了自己
可我仍不住回想,翻来覆去,
一阵无名怒火,让我想把你
从现时的晦暗中　拖拽而出
再摆放进面前的玫瑰花轮,鲜明醒目。
然后,为了肆无忌惮吸取香气,
我碰触到你的利刃,将它紧握,
直到鲜血滴落指缝、汩汩流出
我才终于获得满足。

Katherine Mansfield

[新西兰]凯瑟琳·曼斯菲尔德

1888—1923

凯瑟琳·曼斯菲尔德被称为新西兰文学的奠基人,她的短篇小说为自己带来盛誉。她与中国诗人徐志摩有过一面之缘,并结下友谊。凯瑟琳去世后,徐志摩为她写下《哀曼殊斐儿》一诗。

Butterfly Laughter

In the middle of our porridge plates

There was a blue butterfly painted

And each morning we tried who should reach the butterfly first.

Then the Grandmother said: "Do not eat the poor butterfly."

That made us laugh.

Always she said it and always it started us laughing.

It seemed such a sweet little joke.

I was certain that one fine morning

The butterfly would fly out of the plates,

Laughing the teeniest laugh in the world,

And perch on the Grandmother's lap.

蝴蝶的笑声

在我家粥盘的盘底正中,
有一只彩绘的蓝色蝴蝶。
每天早上我们都要比试,谁先喝光汤底、露出蝴蝶。
这时祖母会说:"别把可怜的蝴蝶吃掉。"
逗得我们哈哈大笑。
每次她都这么说,每次我们都会发笑。
像是个非常甜蜜的小小笑料。
我当时确信,某个美好的清晨,
蝴蝶会振翅飞出盘子、翩跹舞蹈,
笑出世界上最纤细的笑声,
然后栖息在祖母的膝头。

The Awakening River

The gulls are mad-in-love with the river,

And the river unveils her face and smiles.

In her sleep-brooding eyes they mirror their shining wings.

She lies on silver pillows: the sun leans over her.

He warms and warms her, he kisses and kisses her.

There are sparks in her hair and she stirs in laughter.

Be careful, my beautiful waking one! you will catch on fire.

Wheeling and flying with the foam of the sea on their breasts,

The ineffable mists of the sea clinging to their wild wings,

Crying the rapture of the boundless ocean,

The gulls are mad-in-love with the river.

Wake! we are the dream thoughts flying from your heart.

Wake! we are the songs of desire flowing from your bosom.

O, I think the sun will lend her his great wings

And the river will fly away to the sea with the mad-

in-love birds.

苏醒的河流

海鸥疯狂地爱着河流,

河流揭去面纱,展露笑颜。

在她睡意惺忪的清眸里,他们照映着闪亮的双翼。

她仰卧在银枕:太阳向着她俯身。

他给她一片片温暖,他予她一次次亲吻。

她的秀发火花点点,她激发出笑声阵阵。

当心啊,我美丽梦醒的姑娘!你会着火。

胸膛沾着海水的浪沫,它们盘旋翱翔,

狂野的翼缠绕着海水难以言喻的雾气,

啸叫着浩渺无边的海洋的狂喜,

海鸥们疯狂爱恋着河流。

醒来!我们是你心里飞出的梦想。

醒来!我们是你胸中流出的情歌。

哦,我想太阳会借她一双巨大的翅膀

让河流同痴恋的鸟儿一起,飞向海洋。

Voice of the Air

But then there comes that moment rare

When, for no cause that I can find,

The little voices of the air

Sound above all the sea and wind.

The sea and wind do then obey

And sighing, sighing double notes

Of double basses, content to play

A droning chord for the little throats—

The little throats that sing and rise

Up into the light with lovely ease

And a kind of magical, sweet surprise

To hear and know themselves for these—

For these little voices: the bee, the fly,

The leaf that taps, the pod that breaks,

The breeze on the grass-tops bending by,

The shrill quick sound that the insect makes.

空中的叫声

但那时罕见时刻忽然来临
我全然不知什么原因,
空中那些微小的叫声
盖过了所有的海和风。

于是海和风便服从
叹息,叹息着双重的音符
和着双部低音,甘愿用低沉的和弦
为那些小小的喉咙伴奏——

小小的歌喉们唱响、飞升
升入日光里　充满迷人的闲逸
给听到这些并了解它们的人
一种神奇而甜蜜的惊喜——

这些小小的喉咙是:蜜蜂,苍蝇,
轻拍的叶片,爆破的豆荚,
弯腰的草尖上的微风,
昆虫发出的尖锐急促的叫声。

Fairy Tale

Now folds the Tree of Day its perfect flowers,

And every bloom becomes a bud again,

Shut and sealed up against the golden showers

Of bees that hover in the velvet hours...

Now a strain

Wild and mournful blown from shadow towers,

Echoed from shadow ships upon the foam,

Proclaims the Queen of Night.

From their bowers

The dark Princesses fluttering, wing their flight

To their old Mother, in her huge old home.

神话故事

现在将白昼之树的完美花朵合拢,

让每支盛开的花重回蓓蕾,

紧锁　密闭,以抵挡金色阵雨般

悬停在丝绒时分的那群蜜蜂……

现在一支乐曲

自影之塔吹送而来　炽烈而忧伤,

又被影之船反射　回荡在浮沫之上,

宣告着　黑夜女王的降临。

从她们的闺房

黑暗公主们鼓翼而出,振翅飞向

她们的老母亲,她身在老家　那宏伟巨大的地方。

The Quarrel

We stood in the vegetable garden
As angry and cross as could be
'Cause you said you wouldn't beg pardon
For eating my radish at tea.

I said, "I shall go an' tell Mummy.
I hope it is makin' you ill.
I hope you've a pain in your tummy,
And then she will give you a pill."

But you cried out, "Good-bye then—for ever.
Go and play with your silly old toys!
If you think you're so grown up and clever,
I'll run off and play with the Boys."

争吵

我俩站在菜园子里
愤怒气恼到极点
因为你吃了我茶点里的小萝卜
却不肯道歉说对不起。

我说:"我要去告诉妈妈。
我希望它让你生病。
让你的肚子疼痛不安,
然后她就让你吃药丸。"

你却嚷嚷起来:"那再见吧——永远别见。
去玩你那些傻气的玩具破烂!
如果你觉得你成熟又聪明,
我就跑去跟男孩们玩。"

Edna St. Vincent Millay
[美国]埃德娜·圣·文森特·米莱
1892—1950

美国诗人、剧作家埃德娜·米莱被人们称为"女拜伦"和"被放逐的雪莱"。她将十四行诗和传统的抒情诗形式带进了现代美国文学。她年少成名，除了拥有令人折服的诗歌天赋，还擅长朗诵和表演。米莱是位天生的女权主义者，她以叛逆而浪漫的生活方式诠释着爱与自由，同时关心社会政治，是温柔的诗人，也是英勇的战士。

Figs from Thistles

I

My candle burns at both ends;

It will not last the night;

But ah, my foes, and oh, my friends—

It gives a lovely light!

II

Safe upon the solid rock the ugly houses stand:

Come and see my shining palace built upon the sand!

蒺藜中长出的无花果

(一)

我的蜡烛从两头燃烧；

它熬不过一个通宵；

但我的敌人，哦，我的朋友——

这烛光多么美妙！

(二)

安座在磐石之上的丑陋房屋：

来看我建在沙上的宫殿，多么光彩夺目！

I Think I Should Have Loved You Presently

I think I should have loved you presently,
And given in earnest words I flung in jest;
And lifted honest eyes for you to see,
And caught your hand against my cheek and breast;
And all my pretty follies flung aside
That won you to me, and beneath your gaze,
Naked of reticence and shorn of pride,
Spread like a chart my little wicked ways.
I, that had been to you, had you remained,
But one more waking from a recurrent dream,
Cherish no less the certain stakes I gained,
And walk your memory's halls, austere, supreme,
A ghost in marble of a girl you knew
Who would have loved you in a day or two.

我想我应该马上就算爱过你了

我想我应该马上就算爱过你了,
假借玩笑　将挚切的话语轻抛;
抬起真诚的眼睛　以求让你看到,
抓起你的手　贴在我脸颊和胸前;
把我可爱的痴蠢　全部抛在一边
这让我赢得了你,在你注视之下,
我再无沉默保留　被剥夺了骄傲,
调皮的小伎俩　悉数坦露供招。
我会一直那样对你,若你不曾离开,
而当我从反复出现的梦境再度醒来,
将我积攒的得失教训铭记珍藏,
便走过你的记忆大厅,冷峻严肃、倨傲高贵,
像大理石像的幽灵,刻着你认识的女孩模样,
她曾在一两天的时间　就爱上你。

Witch-Wife

She is neither pink nor pale,
And she never will be all mine;
She learned her hands in a fairy-tale,
And her mouth on a valentine.

She has more hair than she needs;
In the sun 'tis a woe to me!
And her voice is a string of coloured beads,
Or steps leading into the sea.

She loves me all that she can,
And her ways to my ways resign;
But she was not made for any man,
And she never will be all mine.

巫　妻

她既不红润也不苍白，
她永远不会全身心属于我；
她在一则童话里演练她的手，
在一位情人那修炼她的嘴。

她的发量远多于所需；
阳光下对我简直是场灾难！
她的声音像是彩色珠串，
或是阶梯　通向海岸。

她爱我　全心全意尽己所能，
她对我百依百顺言听计从；
但她不为任何一个男人而生，
她也永远不会全身心属于我。

Spring

To what purpose, April, do you return again?

Beauty is not enough.

You can no longer quiet me with the redness

Of little leaves opening stickily.

I know what I know.

The sun is hot on my neck as I observe

The spikes of the crocus.

The smell of the earth is good.

It is apparent that there is no death.

But what does that signify?

Not only under ground are the brains of men

Eaten by maggots.

Life in itself

Is nothing,

An empty cup, a flight of uncarpeted stairs.

It is not enough that yearly, down this hill,

April

Comes like an idiot, babbling and strewing flowers.

春

是为了什么，四月，你再度归来？

只有美还不足够。

你再也不能用半开合的

新叶的红晕来让我平静。

我了解自己的内心。

当我观察番红花的花穗时

太阳炽热地晒着我的脖子。

泥土的气息沁人心脾。

一眼望去，那里没有死亡。

但那意味着什么？

不只是人的脑髓正在地下

被蛆虫蛀食。

生命本身

就是虚妄，

一只腹内空空的杯子，一段未铺地毯的楼梯。

四月

它每年都来，还是总嫌不够，

它从山上走下，像个傻瓜，胡言乱语，播散鲜花。

City Trees

The trees along this city street,

Save for the traffic and the trains,

Would make a sound as thin and sweet

As trees in country lanes.

And people standing in their shade

Out of a shower, undoubtedly

Would hear such music as is made

Upon a country tree.

Oh, little leaves that are so dumb

Against the shrieking city air,

I watch you when the wind has come—

I know what sound is there.

城市的树

这城市街道沿途的树木,
除去车辆和火车的噪音,
和乡间小道的树木一样
会发出尖细悦耳的声响。

当人们站在树阴里
躲避阵雨,无疑会听到
和乡村树木上方一样的
这种音乐。

哦,小小的叶片沉默噤声
映衬着尖声喧嚣的城市天空,
当风吹过,我注视着你们——
我知道那是怎样的声音。

Marianne Moore
[美国]玛丽安娜·穆尔
1887-1972

玛丽安娜·穆尔是20世纪美国重要的诗人,她用精确、敏锐的诗歌语言描绘人物、地点、动物和艺术。穆尔曾获普利策诗歌奖和美国国家图书奖。她兴趣广泛,是位狂热的棒球迷。

He Made This Screen

not of silver nor of coral,

but of weather beaten laurel.

Here, he introduced a sea

uniform like tapestry;

here, a fig-tree; there, a face;

there, a dragon circling space —

designating here, a bower;

there, a pointed passion-flower.

他制作了这座屏风

不用银子,也不用珊瑚,
而是用栉风沐雨的月桂树

这里,他引来一片海
均匀伸展如一张织锦;

这里,一颗无花果;那里,一副面孔;
那里,飞龙盘旋的苍穹——

标明这里,搭一座凉亭;
那里,开一朵尖瓣的西番莲。

Roses Only

You do not seem to realise that beauty is a liability
rather than
an asset—that in view of the fact that spirit creates
form we are justified in supposing
that you must have brains. For you, a symbol of the
unit, stiff and sharp,
conscious of surpassing by dint of native superiority
and liking for everything self-dependent, anything
an

ambitious civilisation might produce: for you,
unaided to attempt through sheer
reserve, to confute presumptions resulting from
observation, is idle. You cannot make us
think you a delightful happen-so. But rose, if you
are
brilliant, it is not because your petals are the
without-which-nothing of pre-eminence.
You would look, minus

thorns—like a what-is-this, a mere

peculiarity. They are not proof against a worm, the
elements, or

mildew but what about the predatory hand? What
is brilliance without co-ordination? Guarding the
infinitesimal pieces of your mind, compelling
audience to

the remark that it is better to be forgotten than to
be remembered too violently,

your thorns are the best part of you.

只有玫瑰

你似乎没意识到,美丽是一种负累

而非资本——鉴于精神创造形式这一事实,

我们有理由推断,你必是兰心蕙质。

你,一个聚合的象征,

既僵硬呆板又敏锐机智,

既明了自己得天厚爱的卓越优势

又喜欢一切依靠自己,和任何

雄心勃勃的文明可能产出的东西:

对于你,仅靠拘谨矜持去独立尝试,

对依据观察得来的推想进行驳斥,

都无济于事。你无法让我们相信

你只是一个令人愉悦的偶然巧合。

但是玫瑰,如果说你光彩照人,

不是因为你的花瓣超凡绝艳、足以傲世,

若除去尖刺,你会看起来令人困惑、怪异奇特。

尖刺不能抵挡蛀虫、风雨或霉菌,

但掠夺攀折的手呢？若无配合，哪来魅力四射？
守护你头脑的细微碎片，迫使观众得出意见，

若被记起将遭遇如此暴力，还不如被遗忘，
你的刺　是你最出色的地方。

That Harp You Play so Well

O David, if I had

Your power, I should be glad—

In harping, with the sling,

In patient reasoning!

Blake, Homer, Job, and you,

Have made old wine-skins new.

Your energies have wrought

Stout continents of thought.

But, David, if the heart

Be brass, what boots the art

Of exorcising wrong,

Of harping to a song?

The sceptre and the ring

And every royal thing

Will fail. Grief's lustiness

Must cure that harp's distress.

那竖琴你弹得真好

哦,大卫,如果我拥有
你的力量,我将乐意去
弹奏竖琴,让投石索
在忍耐中推测、猜忌!

布莱克、荷马、约伯和你,
让旧葡萄酒囊更新换代。
你们用精明强干缔造出
坚实如大陆的思想体系。

但是,大卫,若你的心灵
由黄铜铸成,是什么引导了这种艺术,
通过拨弄竖琴　弹奏音乐
可以除魔驱邪?

权杖、指环、
任何王权的东西,
都力不能及。定是悲伤之深厚
消除、疗愈了　竖琴的忧愁。

Those Various Scalpels

Those

various sounds, consistently indistinct, like

intermingled echoes

struck from thin glasses successively at random—

the inflection disguised: your hair, the tails of two

fighting-cocks head to head in stone—

like sculptured scimitars repeating the curve of your

ears in reverse order:

your eyes,

flowers of ice and snow

sown by tearing winds on the cordage of disabled

ships: your

raised hand

an ambiguous signature: your cheeks, those

rosettes

of blood on the stone floors of French châteaux,

with regard to which the guides are so affirmative—

your other hand

a bundle of lances all alike, partly hid by emeralds
from Persia
and the fractional magnificence of Florentine
goldwork—a collection of little objects—
sapphires set with emeralds, and pearls with a
moonstone, made fine
with enamel in gray, yellow, and dragonfly blue;
a lemon, a pear

and three bunches of grapes, tied with silver: your
dress, a magnificent square
cathedral tower of uniform
and at the same time diverse appearance—a
species of vertical vineyard, rustling in the storm
of conventional opinion—are they weapons or
scalpels?
Whetted to brilliance

by the hard majesty of that sophistication which is
superior to opportunity,

these things are rich instruments with which to
experiment.
But why dissect destiny with instruments
more highly specialized than the components of
destiny
itself?

那些各式各样的手术刀

那些
各不相同的声音,始终模糊不清,像混杂的回声
随机地在薄玻璃上连续撞击——
声调的抑扬被掩饰伪装:你的头发,
两只头抵头的斗鸡石像的尾羽——
像雕刻的短弯刀
反向重复你耳朵的弧度线条:
你的眼睛,
冰雪之花

被猛烈的风在残破轮船的绳索上播撒:
你抬起的手,
一个含糊不明的识别标志:你的脸颊,
法国城堡的石质地板上血液凝成的玫瑰花结,
对于此事的指引如此肯定——
你的另一只手

一捆完全相像的长矛,一部分被波斯绿松石
和佛罗伦萨金器那碎片式的富丽堂皇掩盖——

零星几只小物件的集合——

蓝宝石镶着绿松石,珍珠点缀着月光石,

用灰白、淡黄和蜻蜓蓝色的珐琅精工制作的;

一颗柠檬、一只梨

和三串葡萄,以银丝相系:你的衣服,

一座宏伟而守旧的制服大教堂

同时又外观多样——

一方垂直的葡萄园,在传统观念的风暴里

沙沙作响——它们是武器还是手术刀?

无需好运却精明老练地

用严酷的威权　打磨至寒光闪现,

这些昂贵的工具被用于实验。

但为何用比命运本身的组织部分

更高度精细的工具

去解剖命运?

To an Intra-mural Rat

You make me think of many men

Once met, to be forgot again

Or merely resurrected

In a parenthesis of wit

That found them hastening through it

Too brisk to be inspected.

致一只墙内的老鼠

你让我想起很多人
一夕相遇,又被忘记
或仅仅重现于
头脑中的某段插曲
他们从中匆匆闪过
轻快到难以察觉

An Egyptian Pulled Glass Bottle in the Shape of a Fish

Here we have thirst

And patience, from the first,

And art, as in a wave held up for us to see

In its essential perpendicularity;

Not brittle but

Intense-the spectrum, that

Spectacular and nimble animal the fish,

Whose scales turn aside the sun's sword with their

polish.

一个鱼形的埃及拉制玻璃瓶

这里,我们有干渴

与忍耐,始于最初,

还有工艺,参见这朵掀起的浪花

令人可鉴其精髓的垂直度;

并不脆弱易碎　而是

强烈绷紧——这材质,

这条鱼,令人惊叹、灵巧敏捷的动物,

用鳞片的抛光面　闪开了太阳的光剑。

Christina Rossetti

[英国]克丽丝蒂娜·罗塞蒂

1830—1894

克丽丝蒂娜·罗塞蒂被称为英国第一女诗人。罗塞蒂出生在一个文学艺术气息浓厚的家庭,她的诗歌常常以爱情、生命、死亡为主题,细腻唯美,受到各个时代诗人的盛赞。

From Sunset to Star Rise

Go from me, summer friends, and tarry not:
I am no summer friend, but wintry cold,
A silly sheep benighted from the fold,
A sluggard with a thorn-choked garden plot.
Take counsel, sever from my lot your lot,
Dwell in your pleasant places, hoard your gold;
Lest you with me should shiver on the wold,
Athirst and hungering on a barren spot.

For I have hedged me with a thorny hedge,
I live alone, I look to die alone:
Yet sometimes when a wind sighs through the sedge,
Ghosts of my buried years and friends come back,
My heart goes sighing after swallows flown
On sometime summer's unreturning track.

从日落到星起

远离我吧,夏日朋友,切勿逗留:
我可不是夏日朋友,而是寒冬般冷酷,
是愚蠢的羔羊　在羊圈外迷途,
是怠惰的懒汉　任花园荆棘遍布。
听我奉劝,将你的命运与我割离,
住在你的安乐窝里,囤积金子;
免得你跟我在荒原哆嗦战栗,
忍渴受饥　困顿之地一片贫瘠。

因为　我已用刺篱将自己围起,
独自生活,也将孤独老去:
但有时　莎草丛中响起风的叹息,
唤回逝去岁月和友人的残影旧忆,
我的心也叹息踌躇　当燕子飞向
夏天那永无归途的前路。

A Birthday

My heart is like a singing bird
Whose nest is in a watered shoot;
My heart is like an apple-tree
Whose boughs are bent with thick-set fruit;
My heart is like a rainbow shell
That paddles in a halcyon sea;
My heart is gladder than all these
Because my love is come to me.

Raise me a dais of silk and down;
Hang it with vair and purple dyes;
Carve it in doves and pomegranates,
And peacocks with a hundred eyes;
Work it in gold and silver grapes,
In leaves and silver fleurs-de-lys;
Because the birthday of my life
Is come, my love is come to me.

生　日

我的心像只鸣唱的小鸟，

在水嫩的枝桠上筑巢；

我的心像株苹果树，

被累累果实压弯了枝条；

我的心像彩虹色的贝壳，

在平静的海水里游弋；

我的心比这些都更欢快，

因为我的爱人就要到来。

为我筑起铺满丝绸和绒毛的高台；

悬挂上灰鼠皮和紫色织染；

雕刻上鸽子、石榴，

和百眼翎毛的孔雀；

再镶嵌上金银葡萄，

叶子和银鸢尾花饰；

因为我的新生就要到来，

我的爱人正向我走来。

A Summer Wish

Live all thy sweet life through
Sweet Rose, dew-sprent,
Drop down thine evening dew
To gather it anew
When day is bright:
I fancy thou wast meant
Chiefly to give delight.

Sing in the silent sky,
Glad soaring bird;
Sing out thy notes on high
To sunbeam straying by
Or passing cloud;
Heedless if thou art heard
Sing thy full song aloud.

O that it were with me
As with the flower;
Blooming on its own tree

For butterfly and bee

Its summer morns:

That I might bloom mine hour

A rose in spite of thorns.

O that my work were done

As birds' that soar

Rejoicing in the sun:

That when my time is run

And daylight too,

I so might rest once more

Cool with refreshing dew.

夏日心愿

希望你整个人生甜美,

似玫瑰芬芳、露珠点缀,

滴落你夜晚的露水,

待天明以后

再重新凝集:

我猜想你的使命

多半是带来欢喜。

在寂静的天空歌唱,

鸟儿畅快翱翔;

高声唱出你的音符,

向着那迷散飘浮、

随云舒云卷的光束;

别在意是否被听到,

让整首歌响彻云霄。

愿它与我一道

也与花一道;

绽放在自己的树梢

为蝴蝶和蜜蜂轻启

夏日的晨曦:

愿我能生如夏花般绚丽,

似一支玫瑰　不畏荆棘。

哦　我的使命已完成,

像小鸟在阳光里

飞舞欢腾:

当我已时日无多,

日色也稀薄黯淡,

我将与清凉的露水相伴,

再一次　进入长眠。

Echo

Come to me in the silence of the night;
Come in the speaking silence of a dream;
Come with soft rounded cheeks and eyes as bright
As sunlight on a stream;
Come back in tears,
O memory, hope, love of finished years.

O dream how sweet, too sweet, too bitter sweet,
Whose wakening should have been in Paradise,
Where souls brimful of love abide and meet;
Where thirsting longing eyes
Watch the slow door
That opening, letting in, lets out no more.

Yet come to me in dreams, that I may live
My very life again though cold in death:
Come back to me in dreams, that I may give
Pulse for pulse, breath for breath:
Speak low, lean low,
As long ago, my love, how long ago!

回　声

到我这来　在这静谧的深夜；
来吧　伴着梦中无声的呓语；
来吧　带着你柔美的圆脸　和溪流波光般
明亮的双眼；
含着泪水归来吧，
哦　那是逝去岁月的回忆、希望与爱恋。

哦梦多么甜蜜，太甜蜜，甜到苦涩，
梦醒之时　仿若身在天国，
满溢爱情的灵魂在那里等候相会；
渴求期盼的眼睛在那里
看着那扇门缓慢
开启，让人进入，永不能出。

但还是在梦中到我这儿来吧，
我虽尸骨已寒也仍能重新活过：
在梦中回到我身边，让我与你
脉搏换取脉搏，呼吸换取呼吸：
窃窃私语，静静相依，
一如往昔，我的爱人啊，多么久远的往昔！

Another Spring

If I might see another Spring

I'd not plant summer flowers and wait:

I'd have my crocuses at once,

My leafless pink mezereons,

My chill-veined snowdrops, choicer yet

My white or azure violet,

Leaf-nested primrose; anything

To blow at once not late.

If I might see another Spring

I'd listen to the daylight birds

That build their nests and pair and sing,

Nor wait for mateless nightingale;

I'd listen to the lusty herds,

The ewes with lambs as white as snow,

I'd find out music in the hail

And all the winds that blow.

If I might see another Spring—

O stinging comment on my past

That all my past results in "if"—

If I might see another Spring

I'd laugh to-day, to-day is brief;

I would not wait for anything:

I'd use to-day that cannot last,

Be glad to-day and sing.

又一个春天

如果我能看到又一个春天,

我将不再种植并等待夏天的花:

我要马上拥有番红花,

我的无叶粉色瑞香,

不畏霜雪的雪花莲,更想要,

纯白或湛蓝的紫罗兰,

叶片簇生的报春花;任何花

马上开放　不宜迟。

如果我能看到又一个春天

我将去倾听白天的小鸟

搭窝筑巢、成双结对、歌唱鸣叫,

不再等待那单飞的夜莺;

我将去倾听那健壮的羊群,

母羊与洁白如雪的羊羔,

我将从冰雹和所有吹拂的风里

找寻音律。

如果我能看到又一个春天——

哦,对我过往的辛辣点评
将我所有经历归于"如果"——
如果我能看到又一个春天
我今天便要欢笑,今日转瞬即逝;
我绝不为任何事等待:
我要利用这无法延续的今天,
及时行乐,纵情放歌。

"One Foot on Sea, and One on Shore"

"Oh tell me once and tell me twice
And tell me thrice to make it plain,
When we who part this weary day,
When we who part shall meet again."

"When windflowers blossom on the sea
And fishes skim along the plain,
Then we who part this weary day,
Then you and I shall meet again."

"Yet tell me once before we part,
Why need we part who part in pain?
If flowers must blossom on the sea,
Why, we shall never meet again."

"My cheeks are paler than a rose,
My tears are salter than the main,
My heart is like a lump of ice
If we must never meet again."

"Oh weep or laugh, but let me be,

And live or die, for all's in vain;

For life's in vain since we must part,

And parting must not meet again"

"Till windflowers blossom on the sea,

And fishes skim along the plain;

Pale rose of roses let me be,

Your breaking heart breaks mine again."

"一脚踩在海上,一脚踏在岸边"

"哦　跟我说一遍　跟我说两遍
跟我说三遍　说说清楚,
当我们在这疲倦的日子分离,
分离的人何时才能相聚。"

"当银莲花盛开在海面
当鱼儿飞掠平原,
这疲倦之日分离的我们,
你与我才能相见。"

"可离开前　再告诉我一遍,
分离痛苦　我们又何必分离?
如果一定要花开放在海面,
唉,我们永远不能相见。"

"我的脸颊惨白过玫瑰,
我的泪咸过海水,
我的心冻结成冰
如果我们再也不能相会。"

"哦　哭啊笑啊，全都随我去，
生啊死啊，一切徒劳无益；
人生无望　因我们必须分离，
分离之后　相见遥遥无期。

"直到银莲花盛开在海面，
直到鱼儿飞掠平原；
就让我做最惨白的那朵玫瑰，
你分离的心让我再次心碎。"

Sappho

[古希腊]萨福

公元前 620- 公元前 550

古希腊女诗人萨福生于公元前七世纪。她一边弹拨竖琴一边吟唱,她发明的抒情诗歌被称为"萨福体",柏拉图称她为人间的第十位缪斯。美貌、才华、殉情……关于她的传说支离破碎,唯一清晰的是她对爱和美的追逐。

It's no Use / Mother Dear...

It's no use

Mother dear, I

can't finish my

weaving

You may

blame Aphrodite

soft as she is

she has almost

killed me with

love for that boy

没用啊 / 亲爱的妈妈……

没用啊

亲爱的妈妈,
我无法完成
我的编织
你就怪
阿芙洛狄忒吧

她如此温柔

却几乎要
用我对那男孩的爱
置我于死地

注:

　　Aphrodite(阿芙洛狄忒),古希腊神话中的女神,象征爱欲和女性美。

As Wind Upon the Mountain Oaks

As wind upon the mountain oaks in storm,
So Eros shakes my soul, my life, my form.

像狂风撼动橡树

像狂风撼动山间的橡树,

厄洛斯撼动我的灵魂、我的生命、我的身体。

注:

　　Eros(厄洛斯),古希腊神话中的爱神。

One Girl

I

Like the sweet apple which reddens upon the topmost bough,
Atop on the topmost twig, — which the pluckers forgot, somehow, —
Forget it not, nay; but got it not, for none could get it till now.

II

Like the wild hyacinth flower which on the hills is found,
Which the passing feet of the shepherds for ever tear and wound,
Until the purple blossom is trodden in the ground.

一位少女

(一)

像一枚甜美的苹果,在最高的枝条,

最顶处细枝上变红——却不知为何,被采摘者忘却,——

不,未曾忘却;但不可得,至今无人能折。

(二)

像山坡上寻到的野风信子,

被牧人的脚步一再划伤撕扯,

直到这姹紫的花被践踏在地面,狼藉一片。

Aphrodite's Doves

When the drifting gray of the vesper shadow
Dimmed their upward path through the midmost azure,
And the length of night overtook them distant
Far from Olympus;

Far away from splendor and joy of Paphos,[1]
From the voice and smile of their peerless Mistress,
Back to whom their truant wings were in rapture
Speeding belated;

Chilled at heart and grieving they drooped their pinions,
Circled slowly, dipping in flight toward Lesbos,[2]
Down through dusk that darkened on Mitylene's[3]
Columns of marble;

Down through glory wan of the fading sunset,

Veering ever toward the abode of Sappho,
Toward my home, the fane of the glad devoted
Slave of the Goddess;

Soon they gained the tile of my roof and rested,
Slipped their heads beneath their wings while I watched them
Sink to sleep and dreams, in the warm and drowsy
Night of midsummer.

阿芙洛狄忒的鸽子

当黄昏的阴翳那飘动的暗影，
模糊了青空中它们向上的路径，
漫长的黑夜已然降临，奥林匹斯
还山高路远。

远离帕福斯的光辉与欢欣，
远离他们无双的女主人的音容笑颜，
归飞的翅膀在狂喜中凌乱，
行速姗姗。

心中凄凉哀伤　它们低垂着羽翼，
缓慢盘旋　飞往莱斯博斯岛屿，
穿越日暮　这暮色荫蔽了米蒂利尼的
大理石柱；

穿越消逝的落日的余晖，
始终朝向萨福的住所，
朝向我的家，一座虔信这位女神的
奴隶的庙宇。

很快　它们落在我屋瓦上憩息，
在我的注视下，把头埋进翅膀，
沉入梦乡，在这温熏而催眠的
仲夏夜晚。

注：

①Paphos，帕福斯，塞浦路斯西南海滨城市，相传阿芙洛狄忒诞生于此处海滩岩石间的浪花泡沫之中。

②Lesbos，莱斯博斯岛，希腊爱琴海中的一个岛屿，为诗人萨福居住地。

③Mitylene，米蒂利尼，位于莱斯博斯岛的东南部，为该岛屿的首府。

Leda

Once on a time

They say that Leda found

Beneath the thyme

An egg upon the ground;

And yet the swan

She fondled long ago

Was whiter than

Its shell of peeping snow.

丽 达

曾经

他们说　丽达发现

百里香下

地面上　有蛋一颗；

而很久以前

她爱抚的那只天鹅

洁白胜过

那皎如雪的蛋壳。

注：

　　Leda（丽达），传说为斯巴达王后，宙斯爱慕其美貌，化作天鹅引诱她，使她生下了著名美人海伦。

Sara Teasdale

[美国]萨拉·提斯黛尔

1884—1933

萨拉·提斯黛尔是 20 世纪初美国的抒情诗人,普利策诗歌奖的首位获得者。在她崭露头角的年代,庞德和艾略特也没有她受欢迎。她是位细腻、孱弱的女诗人,擅长描写女性的情思,笔触华丽、凄美,让人动容。

Let It Be Forgotten

Let it be forgotten, as a flower is forgotten,

Forgotten as a fire that once was singing gold,

Let it be forgotten for ever and ever,

Time is a kind friend, he will make us old.

If anyone asks, say it was forgotten

Long and long ago,

As a flower, as a fire, as a hushed footfall

In a long forgotten snow.

忘记它

忘记它,像忘记一朵花,

忘记一团曾欢唱金色曲调的火,

忘记它　永远永远,

时间是个宽厚的朋友,他带领我们走向老朽。

如果有人问起,就说它已被遗忘

距如今年深日长,

像一朵花,一团火,一个缄默的足迹

深埋在久已遗忘的雪里。

What Do I Care

What do I care, in the dreams and the languor of spring,
That my songs do not show me at all?
For they are a fragrance, and I am a flint and a fire,
I am an answer, they are only a call.

But what do I care, for love will be over so soon,
Let my heart have its say and my mind stand idly by,
For my mind is proud and strong enough to be silent,
It is my heart that makes my songs, not I.

我有何在意

我有何在意，在春日的睡梦和慵懒里，
只因我的歌完全没有展现自己？
因为它们是香气，而我是火石与火焰，
我是回答，它们只是呼唤。

但我有何在意，爱情如过眼云烟飘散，
让我的心来决定，让头脑靠边闲站，
因为我的头脑骄傲坚强，足以沉默不言，
是我的心造就了我的歌，而不是我。

Only in Sleep

Only in sleep I see their faces,
Children I played with when I was a child,
Louise comes back with her brown hair braided,
Annie with ringlets warm and wild.

Only in sleep Time is forgotten—
What may have come to them, who can know?
Yet we played last night as long ago,
And the doll-house stood at the turn of the stair.

The years had not sharpened their smooth round faces,
I met their eyes and found them mild—
Do they, too, dream of me, I wonder,
And for them am I too a child?

只在睡梦中

只在睡梦中,我看到她们的面孔,
那些我儿时一起玩耍的孩童,
路易丝回来了,扎着棕色发辫,
安妮满头卷发,狂野而又温暖。

只有在睡梦中,时间才被忘记——
她们后来过得怎样,谁又能够预测?
但昨晚我们一起玩,就像很久以前,
楼梯的转角处,是那间玩偶屋。

岁月没有消磨她们光洁圆润的容颜,
我看到她们的眼睛,眼神温柔和善——
是否她们,也会梦见我,我忍不住猜,
是否对于她们,我也还是个小孩?

The Mystery

Your eyes drink of me,
Love makes them shine,
Your eyes that lean
So close to mine.

We have long been lovers,
We know the range
Of each other's moods
And how they change;

But when we look
At each other so
Then we feel
How little we know;

The spirit eludes us,
Timid and free—
Can I ever know you
Or you know me?

秘 密

你的双眼啜饮着我,
爱让它们闪烁,
你的眼睛朝我倾侧,
距离我的眼睛那么近。

我们已相爱很久,
知道彼此情绪的
波动范围与忍受界限
以及它们如何改变。

但当我们深情地
彼此相望,
我们就会感到
对对方所知甚少。

灵魂对我们遮掩躲避,
羞怯又游离——
你到底能否认识我
我又能否了解你?

May Day

A delicate fabric of bird song

Floats in the air,

The smell of wet wild earth

Is everywhere.

Red small leaves of the maple

Are clenched like a hand,

Like girls at their first communion

The pear trees stand.

Oh I must pass nothing by

Without loving it much,

The raindrop try with my lips,

The grass with my touch;

For how can I be sure

I shall see again

The world on the first of May

Shining after the rain?

五朔节

鸟儿歌声的精妙织物
在空气中飘浮,
野外泥土的湿润气息
弥漫所到之处。

枫树小巧的红色叶片
像手掌握紧的拳,
梨花满树雪白站立
像初领圣体礼的女孩。

哦　路过的每件事物
都让我无限欢喜,
雨滴舔舐我的双唇,
青草摩挲我的肌肤。

我如何能够确信
自己能再次看到
五月一日的世界
在雨后光芒中闪耀?

Thoughts

When I am all alone
Envy me most,
Then my thoughts flutter round me
In a glimmering host;

Some dressed in silver,
Some dressed in white,
Each like a taper
Blossoming light;

Most of them merry,
Some of them grave,
Each of them lithe
As willows that wave;

Some bearing violets,
Some bearing bay,
One with a burning rose
Hidden away—

When I am all alone

Envy me then,

For I have better friends

Than women and men.

想　法

当我一人独处

才最值得嫉妒，

我的想法在四周飘落，

纷纷扬扬、微光闪烁；

一部分穿银，

一部分着白，

像一柄柄细长的蜡烛

将光芒吐露；

大多数是愉快的，

也有的很严肃，

似根根柔韧的柳枝，

它们随风飘舞；

有的长出紫罗兰，

有的生出月桂，

一个在隐秘的角落

开出灼灼明亮的玫瑰——

当我一人独处，

确实值得羡慕，

因为我有妙友相陪，

胜过男女伙伴。

Elinor Wylie
[美国]埃莉诺·怀利
1885—1928

埃莉诺·怀利,美国诗人、小说家。她的诗歌雅致精巧、意象优美。埃莉诺以美貌、才华和丰富的感情生活引人注目,被称为"诗人之中的诗人和王后"。

The Lion and the Lamb

I saw a Tiger's golden flank,
I saw what food he ate,
By a desert spring he drank;
The Tiger's name was Hate.

Then I saw a placid Lamb
Lying fast asleep;
Like a river from its dam
Flashed the Tiger's leap.

I saw a Lion tawny-red,
Terrible and brave;
The Tiger's leap overhead
Broke like a wave.

In sand below or sun above
He faded like a flame.
The Lamb said, "I am Love";
"Lion, tell your name."

The Lion's voice thundering

Shook his vaulted breast,

"I am Love. By this spring,

Brother, let us rest."

狮子与羔羊

我看见一只老虎的侧腹,
我看见他吃的食物,
他在沙漠的泉水边舐饮;
老虎的名字,叫作仇恨。

接着我看见一只驯良的羔羊
在酣睡中卧躺;
像河水冲出堤坝
老虎闪眼间飞跃其上。

我看见一只茶红的狮子,
勇猛刚劲、威风八面;
让跃上头顶的老虎
如浪花一样消散。

像掩埋沙下　或迎上太阳
他黯然泯灭　如一团火光。
羔羊说,"我是爱";
"狮子,请告知我姓名。"

狮子的声音似雷鸣作响,
抖动着它隆起的胸膛,
"我就是爱。来这泉边,
兄弟,我们一起安眠。"

Sunset on the Spire

All that I dream

By day or night

Lives in that stream

Of lovely light.

Here is the earth,

And there is the spire;

This is my hearth,

And that is my fire.

From the sun's dome

I am shouted proof

That this is my home,

And that is my roof.

Here is my food,

And here is my drink,

And I am wooed

From the moon's brink.

And the days go over,

And the nights end;

Here is my lover,

Here is my friend.

All that I

Could ever ask

Wears that sky

Like a thin gold mask.

尖塔上的日落

我梦寐以求

日思夜想,

是在迷人的良夜

宿在那碧溪之上。

这是土地,

那是尖塔;

这是我的壁炉,

那是我的炉火。

在太阳的穹顶

我高呼力证

这是我的家宅,

那是我的屋顶。

这是我所食,

这是我所饮,

我被追逐痴缠,

以月亮为边界起点。

白昼更迭,

夜晚终结;

这是我的爱人,

这是我的朋友。
我所能求的
只此无他：
披上那片天空，
像一层金色的薄纱

Escape

When foxes eat the last gold grape,
And the last white antelope is killed,
I shall stop fighting and escape
Into a little house I'll build.

But first I'll shrink to fairy size,
With a whisper no one understands,
Making blind moons of all your eyes,
And muddy roads of all your hands.

And you may grope for me in vain
In hollows under the mangrove root,
Or where, in apple-scented rain,
The silver wasp-nests hang like fruit.

逃 跑

当狐狸吃掉最后一颗金葡萄,
当最后一只白羚羊被杀戮,
我将停止抗争,逃入
我搭建的小屋。

但首先,我会收缩成精灵的身量,
念起无人能解的低语,
造出月亮,让你们眼睛所到之处一片目盲,
变出小路,令你们触手所及之处遍地泥浆。

或许你们会徒劳地摸索着寻找我,
在红树根须下的浅坑,
或是,那苹果味的雨里,
果实一样挂着的银巢,里面住着黄蜂。

Silver Filigree

The icicles wreathing
On trees in festoon
Swing, swayed to our breathing:
They're made of the moon.

She's a pale, waxen taper;
And these seem to drip
Transparent as paper
From the flame of her tip.

Molten, smoking a little,
Into crystal they pass;
Falling, freezing, to brittle
And delicate glass.

Each a sharp-pointed flower,
Each a brief stalactite
Which hangs for an hour
In the blue cave of night.

银丝饰品

冰柱环绕的树上
装饰着垂花彩灯,
随着我们的呼吸来回摇动:
它们是那月儿做成。

月儿是素淡蜡白的细烛;
而这些冰柱,像是
从她火苗跳跃的顶端滴落的
薄纸般透亮的泪珠凝出。

它们消融,伴着几缕轻烟,
化作莹澈的水晶;
下落、冻结,就成了
精致易碎的琉璃。

每根都是支花苞、才露尖角,
每根都是枚钟乳、短如春梦,
在夜晚的深蓝洞穴上方
悬垂个一时半晌。

Velvet Shoes

Let us walk in the white snow

In a soundless space;

With footsteps quiet and slow,

At a tranquil pace,

Under veils of white lace.

I shall go shod in silk,

And you in wool,

White as a white cow's milk,

More beautiful

Than the breast of a gull.

We shall walk through the still town

In a windless peace;

We shall step upon white down,

Upon silver fleece,

Upon softer than these.

We shall walk in velvet shoes:

Wherever we go

Silence will fall like dews

On white silence below.

We shall walk in the snow.

天鹅绒鞋

让我们踏着白雪

在无声无息的旷野行走;

脚步舒缓而轻柔,

迈着沉静的步伐,

披着洁白的蕾丝面纱。

我要穿着绸缎的鞋子,

你穿羊毛的,

如白牛的乳汁般白,

比白鸥的胸膛

还要光洁漂亮。

我们要走过寂静的小镇

伴着无风的安宁气氛;

我们要踩着洁白的羽绒,

银亮的羊绒,

和更加柔软的东西。

我们要穿着天鹅绒鞋子走路:

无论走到何处，

静谧就像露珠

飘落在纯白的静谧之上。

我们要踏雪而行。

The Persian Kitten

Lie still, my love, and do not speak, because

In silence is fulfilling of these laws;

Fastidious sorcery lives not in speech.

Let each devoutly take the hand of each,

But lightly, and without the emphasis

Of pressure, or persuasion of a kiss.

Breathe now with breath diminished to the least;

Narrow your eyelids to entreat the beast;

Make soft your glances; never show surprise

Discovering the lion in his eyes —

The little lion like a burning bush —

Approaching languidly, with bush and bush

Sighed from the padding velvet, see him crouch

And spurn the carpet for the painted couch,

Like a gilt feather on its pillows tossed.

Lie still, my love, lie still, or all is lost.

From violence of lust remote, withdrawn,

He shudders delicately to a yawn,

And with their pulses in a mute accord

Lies down between these lovers like a sword.

波斯猫

静静躺着,我的爱人,不要说话,
因为在安静中才能满足这些守则;
难于取悦的挑剔魔法　不依靠言语存活。
让我们虔诚地拿起彼此的手,
但轻轻地,别用力施压强调,
也别用亲吻说服劝告。

现在,将呼吸降至最微弱轻柔;
眯起你的眼睛,向这头小兽乞求;
让目光变柔和;
当你从他眼中发现了狮子——
像燃烧的灌木丛般的小狮子——
千万别显露惊讶

待一丛丛灌木慢悠悠靠近,
在软垫的丝绒上叹息,看着他蹲下
摒弃了地毯　跃上彩色沙发,
将自己轻掷靠枕　像镀金羽毛一根。

静静躺着,我的爱人,静静躺着,不然一切尽毁。

从遥远的暴力和欲望中撤回,
他微微颤抖　打了个哈欠,
便躺倒在爱人中间　像一把剑
他们的脉搏　化作静默的和弦。